AN ENERGY EXPERT AT HOME

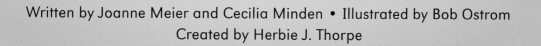

Written by Joanne Meier and Cecilia Minden • Illustrated by Bob Ostrom
Created by Herbie J. Thorpe

ABOUT THE AUTHORS

Joanne Meier, PhD, has worked as an elementary school teacher, university professor, and researcher. She earned her BA in early childhood education from the University of South Carolina, and her MEd and PhD in education from the University of Virginia. She currently works as a literacy consultant for schools and private organizations. Joanne lives in Virginia with her husband Eric, daughters Kella and Erin, two cats, and a gerbil.

Cecilia Minden, PhD, is the former director of the Language and Literacy Program at the Harvard Graduate School of Education. She is now a reading consultant for school and library publications. She earned her PhD in reading education from the University of Virginia. Cecilia and her husband, Dave Cupp, live outside Chapel Hill, North Carolina. They enjoy sharing their love of reading with their grandchildren, Chelsea and Qadir.

ABOUT THE ILLUSTRATOR

Bob Ostrom has been illustrating children's books for nearly twenty years. A graduate of the New England School of Art & Design at Suffolk University, Bob has worked for such companies as Disney, Nickelodeon, and Cartoon Network. He lives in North Carolina with his wife Melissa and three children, Will, Charlie, and Mae.

ABOUT THE SERIES CREATOR

Herbie J. Thorpe had long envisioned a beginning-readers' series about a fun, energetic bear with a big imagination. Herbie is a book lover and an avid supporter of libraries and the role they play in fostering the love of reading. He consults with librarians and matches them with the perfect books for their students and patrons. He lives in Louisiana with his wife Misty and their daughter Carson.

The Child's World

Published in the United States of America by The Child's World®
1980 Lookout Drive • Mankato, MN 56003-1705
800-599-READ • www.childsworld.com

Acknowledgments
The Child's World®: Mary Berendes, Publishing Director
The Design Lab: Kathleen Petelinsek, Design;
Kari Tobin, Page Production
Artistic Assistant: Richard Carbajal

Library of Congress Cataloging-in-Publication Data
Meier, Joanne D.
   An energy expert at home / by Joanne Meier and Cecilia Minden ;
illustrated by Bob Ostrom.
      p. cm. — (Herbster readers)
   ISBN 978-1-60253-226-7 (library bound : alk. paper)
   [1. Energy conservation—Fiction. 2. Bears—Fiction.] I. Minden,
Cecilia. II. Ostrom, Bob, ill. III. Title. IV. Series.

PZ7.M5148Ene 2009
[E]—dc22   2009004005

"Herbie, what are you doing?" asked Mom.

"I'm taping the refrigerator door shut," said Herbie Bear. "Keeping it closed will help us save energy."

"Saving energy is a great idea, Herbie,"
said Mom. "But how can we make dinner
tonight if the refrigerator is closed?"

4

"Oh, gosh," said Herbie. "I didn't think of that."

A little while later, the family sat down to dinner.
"What did you learn in school today?" asked Dad.

6

Herbie was the first to answer. "Science is so cool, Dad! We're learning all about energy."

"An energy expert came and talked to our class.
She taught us different ways to save energy."

"She had a poster that showed how much energy things use. You'd be amazed, Dad!" said Herbie.

"Is that right?" Dad laughed.

"Well, your mom and I have some idea of how much energy we use around here. We're reminded every time the electricity bill comes."

"Mr. Stone gave us a family project,"
explained Herbie. "For one month,
we should try some energy-saving tips."

"I'll write down things we do in this notebook. At the end of the month, our class will plant a tree to celebrate."

"Plant a tree?" asked Hank.
"Why would you plant a tree?"

"If we create more shade for our school, the air conditioner won't have to work as hard," explained Herbie.

"Herbie," said Mom, "I'm glad you're so excited about saving energy."

"Why don't you help us learn some things we can do around the house?"

"Sure!" said Herbie. He led
everyone to the laundry room.

"We can wash our clothes with cold water. Our clothes will get just as clean, and we'll use less energy. We don't have to heat up all that water!"

Next, Herbie led the family to the living room.
"We can turn off the lights when we leave a
room," he said.

"We should turn off the TV and video games when we're done, too," said Herbie.

Herbie went to the window and closed it. "Air escapes through doors and windows," he said.

"When the air conditioner or furnace is running, our windows should be shut. They should be tightly sealed, too."

Herbie led everyone to the bathroom.

"It takes a lot of water to fill up a bathtub," he said.
"Taking short showers uses much less water."

"We don't have to take baths?" asked Hank. "Yippee!"

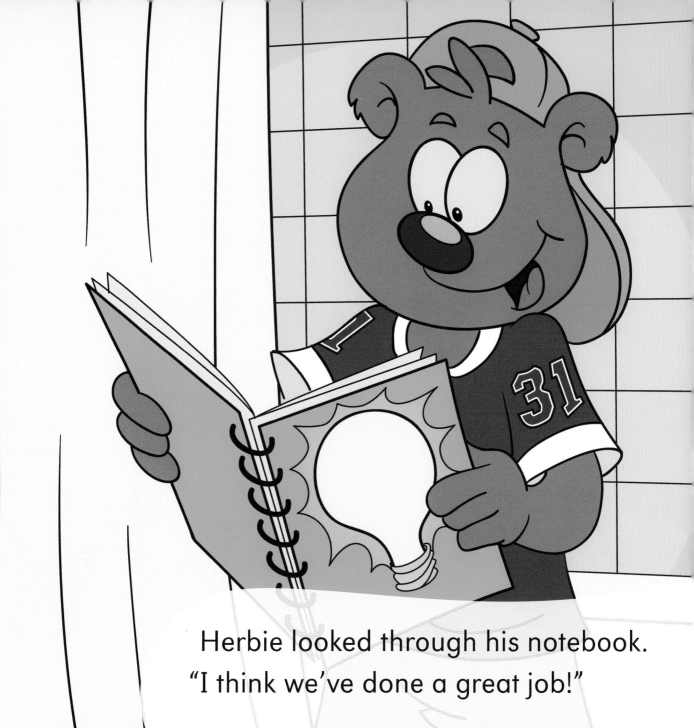

Herbie looked through his notebook.
"I think we've done a great job!"

"We used less hot water," said Mom.

"We turned off lights and TVs," said Hannah.

"We sealed our windows," said Dad.

"We took short showers!" giggled Hank.

Herbie just smiled.